P9-EDX-626

3 1833 01 10 9232

TINY TURTLE'S THANKSGIVING

DAVE ROSS

William Morrow and Company, Inc. / New York

Copyright © 1986 by Dave Ross
All rights reserved. No part of this book may be reproduced or utilized in any form or by any means, electronic or mechanical, including photocopying, recording or by any information storage and retrieval system, without permission in writing from the Publisher. Inquiries should be addressed to William Morrow and Company, Inc., 105 Madison Avenue, New York, NY 10016.

Printed in Hong Kong. 1 2 3 4 5 6 7 8 9 10

Library of Congress Cataloging-in-Publication Data   Ross, Dave, 1949–   Tiny Turtle's Thanksgiving.

Summary: Tired of being a turtle, Tiny Turtle decides to try to be an eagle one Thanksgiving Day, but decides it isn't much fun.

[1. Turtles—Fiction.   2. Thanksgiving Day—Fiction]   I. Title.

PZ7.R71964Ti   1986   [E]   86-5412

ISBN 0-688-06440-X
ISBN 0-688-06441-8 (lib. bdg.)

For Mackenzie

"It's Thanksgiving Day,"
says Papa Turtle.

"Today we will feast
on stuffed stinkbug
and give thanks
for everything,"
adds Mama Turtle.

"But I'm not thankful for everything.
I'm tired of eating stinkbugs,
and I don't like being a turtle."

"I'd rather be an eagle."

"Then why not try
to be an eagle?"

FLAP!

FLAP!

FLAP!

SPLAT!

"Maybe starting a little higher will help."

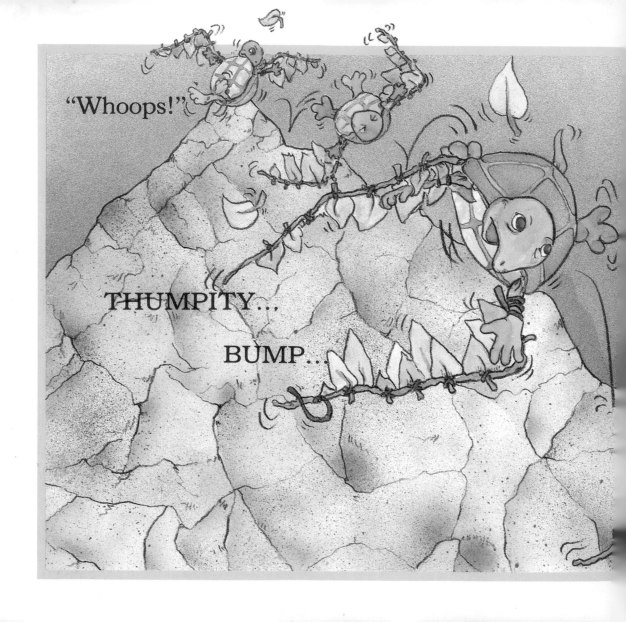

PLOP!

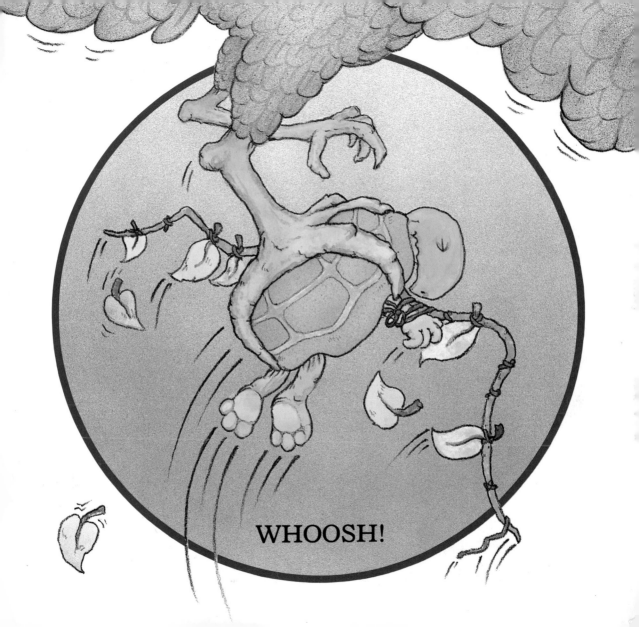

WHOOSH!

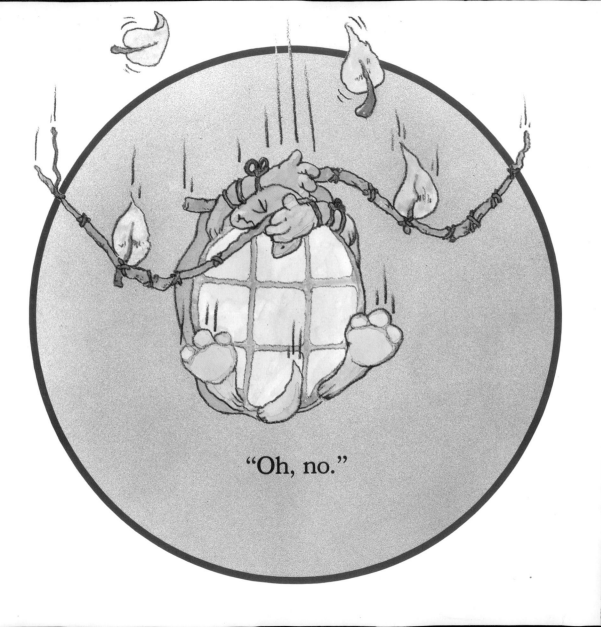

"Oh, no."

"Maybe it's not so bad
to be a turtle after all."